ELEPHANT GAMES

AND OTHER PLAYFUL POEMS TO PERFORM

Text copyright ©1995 by Brod Bagert
Illustrations copyright ©1995 by Tim Ellis
All rights reserved

Published by Wordsong
Boyds Mills Press, Inc.
A Highlights Company
815 Church Street
Honesdale, Pennsylvania 18431
Printed in China

Publisher Cataloging-in-Publication Data
Bagert, Brod.
   Elephant games : and other playful poems / by Brod Bagert.
[32]p. : col. ill. ; cm.
Summary : Humorous poems for children.
ISBN 1-56397-293-X hc / ISBN 1-56397-862-8 pbk
1. Humorous poetry—Juvenile literature. 2. Children's poetry, American.
[1. Humorous poetry. 2. American poetry.] I. Title.
811.54—dc20   1995   CIP
Library of Congress Catalog Card Number 94-73319

First Boyds Mills Press paperback edition, 2000
Book designed by Tim Gillner
The text of this book is set in 16-point Palatino
The illustrations are done in watercolors and colored pencils.

10 9 8 7 6 5 4 3 2 1

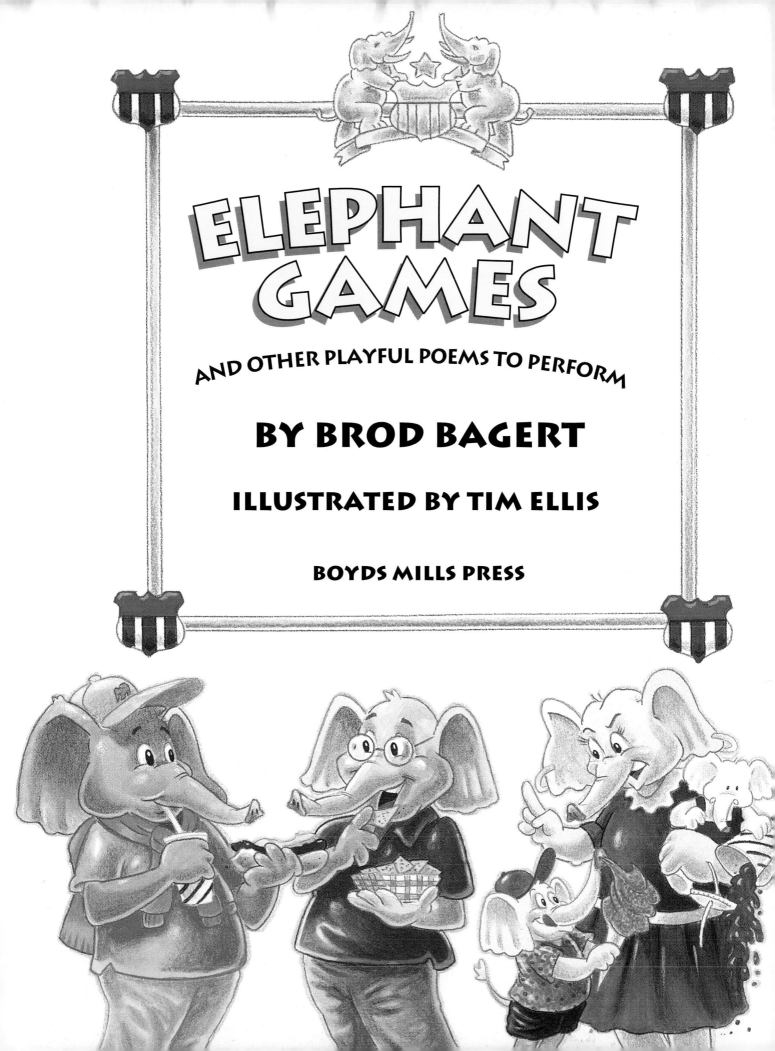

ELEPHANT GAMES

AND OTHER PLAYFUL POEMS TO PERFORM

BY BROD BAGERT

ILLUSTRATED BY TIM ELLIS

BOYDS MILLS PRESS

To Katherine Kerne
The original country grandmother

—B.B.

To Mom & Dad
Thanks for the gift of your love, hardwork,
and dedication in raising a great family!
You've given me a wonderful life!

—T.E.

Contents

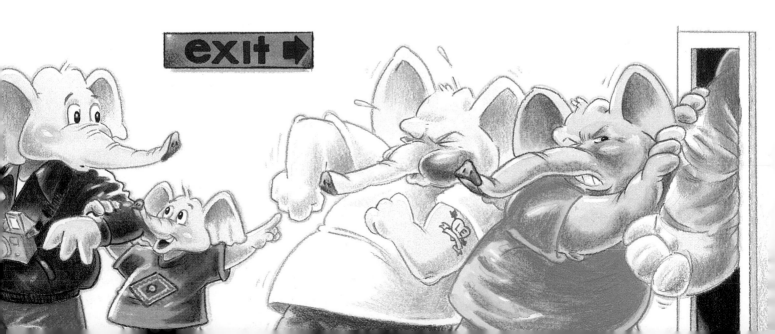

Elephant Games

Some elephants live inside my ear
And they make it very hard to hear.

In the morning they stomp their elephant feet
Until I give them sweets to eat.

When things at school get a little boring,
They fill my nose with elephant snoring.

Then late at night when I lie in bed,
I hear elephant games inside my head.

It's really true, it's not an invention.
That's why it's so hard to get my attention.

So when Mom talks and I don't hear
It's because of those elephants in my ear.

The Hundreth Day of School

Kindergarten's kids' stuff
But first grade's a giant change
So when I started school that day
My stomach felt real strange.

The classroom was green,
The teacher looked mean,
I didn't have a single friend.
And time went by so slow
I thought that day would never end.

I was just a kid back then,
But now I'm wise in many ways.
It's amazing how much things can change
In just a hundred days.

Little League Magic

The rabbit's foot inside my hat
Got me a hit each time at bat.

This morning I used my lucky comb,
That's why I slid in safe at home.

I didn' t wash my socks today
So my glove was hot on every play.

But instead of being happy
All I feel is sorrow.

Oh sure my magic worked today,
But will it work tomorrow?

The Tadpole's Dream

When I hatched in the water
I looked like a fish,
But there in the pond
I felt a strange wish.

Someday . . . some way . . .
I will live on the land.
I'm not quite sure how
But I'm sure that I can.
My body will change,
Someday soon it will start,
I can feel it inside me
Deep deep in my heart.

I never gave up
And one spring day I found
I'd grown arms and long legs
So I hopped on the ground.

And now I eat flies,
I bask in the sun
With big blinky eyes
In a world full of fun.

But I always remember
The Big Bullfrog Rule:
> *When a kid comes to catch you*
> *Jump back in the pool.*

11

The Wall

I look at the stars on a winter night
Each one in its proper place,
And wonder how can it possibly be
That there is no end to space?
There must be an end . . . a giant wall,
I finally decide.
Then I wonder again,
If there is such a wall,
Then what's on the other side?

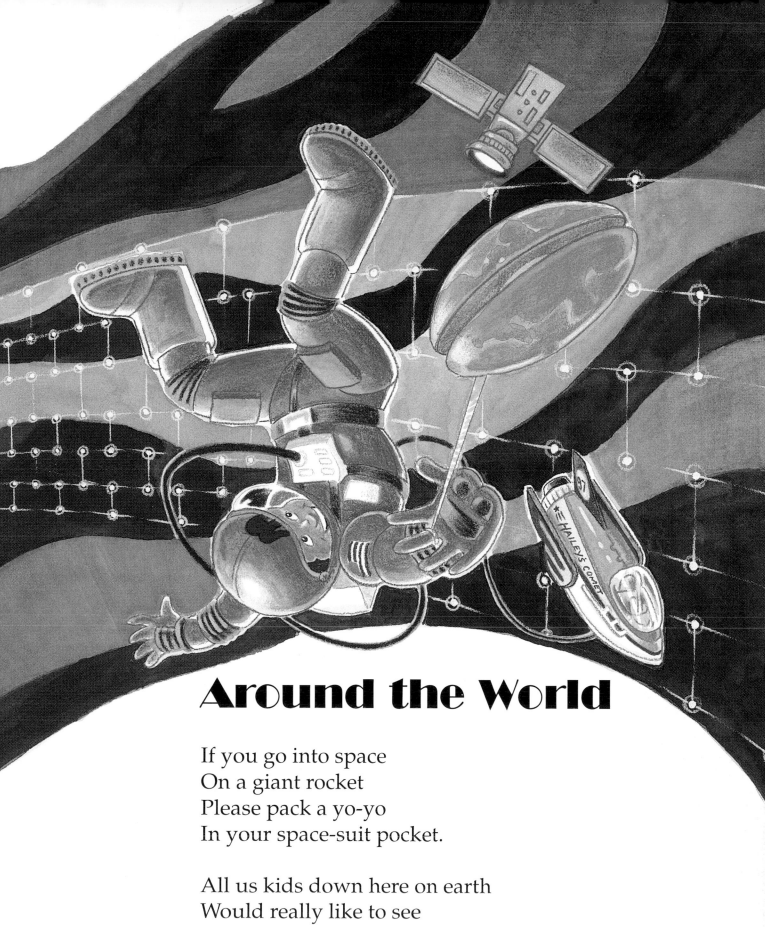

Around the World

If you go into space
On a giant rocket
Please pack a yo-yo
In your space-suit pocket.

All us kids down here on earth
Would really like to see
An astronaut do yo-yo tricks
Afloat in zero "G."

13

Big Trouble

No free time for me.
I'm in trouble now.
I try to be good
But I don't know how.

First I talked out of turn,
Then I ran in the hall,
Then I bopped Billy Burns
On the head with a ball.

"Keep your hands to yourself,"
I heard Ms. Schmidt say,
"Your name's on the board
And that's where it will stay."

I try to be good,
But I just don't know how.
So my name's on the board.
I'm in big trouble now.

The Eraser

I made a lot of mistakes today.
Twelve minus five does not equal eight.
Carrot does not start with a K.
And *"No, stupid, you cannot sit next to me!"*
Was not a nice thing to say.

I erased the eight and wrote seven.
I erased the K and wrote C.
But nothing can erase the tears
You cried because of me.

So I wrote this little poem
To find a way to say,
I'm sorry.
Please forgive me
For hurting you today.

The Night I Caught the Burglar

Last night I heard a funny noise
While I was in my bed,
And wondered, "Should I take a peek,
Or go back to sleep instead?"
I got out of bed,
Put my feet on the floor,
As quiet as a mouse,
And made my way from room to room
In a dark and scary house.
Then I saw a burglar,
All dressed up in black,
He'd taken all my toys
And stuffed them in a sack.
I jumped right out and shouted STOP!
I pushed him to the floor.
I held him till the policemen came
And led him out the door.
It felt so nice to be so brave,
My Mom and Dad were beaming!
But then the clock began to ring—
Oh shucks! I was just dreaming.

Country Grandmother

My grandma lives in the country,
And you'd think she loves to cook,
To make thick fudge and apple pies,
In a rocking chair with failing eyes,
Smiling sweet, hair silver gray
You'd think she knits and sews all day.

Well you'd be wrong.
She never cooks.
She never learned to sew.
And grandma never sits around,
She's always on the go.

My grandma jogs at the crack of dawn
And mows her own two-acre lawn.
Reads current books
Attends college classes
And wears rhinestones
In her bifocal glasses.

She recently turned seventy
But she's always on the run,
And she says when she's a hundred
She'll still be having fun.

Children of the Sun

Mercury's small,
Almost nothing at all.

Venus is bright and near.

Earth is a planet with deep blue seas
And a sky that's blue and clear.

Mars is red and angry.

Jupiter has an eye.

Saturn has rings of ice and stone
That circle around its sky.

Uranus, Neptune, and Pluto
Are far away and cold.

So now I know my planets,
And I'm only eight years old.

Daytime Sleeper

My hamster snoozes all day long
And plays at night while I sleep.
What foolish hours to keep!
I tell him what's right,
He should sleep at night,
But in spite of my constant warning,
At night he runs around in his wheel
And goes to sleep in the morning.

NO

You'll hear it every day.
It's how they teach the rules.

NO, you cannot stay in bed today
Get up and dress for school.

NO, you'll have to wait for recess.

NO, don't bite your nails.

NO, the lunchroom's not the place
To braid your ponytails.

NO you can't go out to play.

NO cookies.

NO ice cream.

NO, it's time for homework.

It's enough to make you scream.

They sure do like that "NO."
They use it day and night.
I just wish I could teach them
The way to use it right.

NO need to make your bed today.

NO homework for a week.

NO more chores.

NO locked doors.

NO time when kids can't speak.

NO nasty don'ts.

NO never do's.

NO Sunday clothes.

NO pickle stews.

It's not a bad word after all
If you don't abuse it.
It all depends whose mouth it's in
And how they're gonna use it.

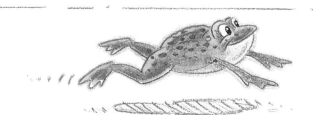

Yellow for Frog
Red for Alligator

In the swamp at night
When you shine your light
At two red eyes sitting on a log . . .
Beware! Beware!
The creature there
Is bigger than a frog.

Slowpoke

I see you slimy slowpoke snail
As you leave your shiny silver trail,
Sliding over rocks and stone,
Your eyes on poles,
Your shell like bone.

I cannot stay here all day long,
You move so slow! Is something wrong?
I'd like to watch your lazy show,
But Mom just called,
It's time to go.

The Big Pout

I got so mad I held my breath.
I got so mad I stubbed my toe.
I got so mad I ran away
But found there was no place to go.

My friends called up,
The neighbors came,
My parents thought they were to blame.
Doctors poked
And lawyers joked,
But still my mood remained the same.

I stayed that way from May the third
Until the fifth of December,
When somebody asked me, "Why are you mad?"
And I smiled, "I don't remember."

26

True Love

Flies and worms and snails and frogs,
Rats and germs and snakes and hogs,
Spiders crawling up your spine.
Won't you be my Valentine?

Milk

I love my milk at breakfast
With Rice Krispies and Corn Flakes.
I mix it up with chocolate
And make yummy chocolate shakes.

I like it cold with supper
And when night things start to creep
I like it nice and warm in bed
To help me go to sleep.

It's not like Coke or 7UP.
They make it white
But I'm not sure how.
All I know for certain is
They start off with a cow.

Jennifer's Secret

They were mean to her at school,
She hadn't been there very long
And everything she tried to do
Seemed to turn out wrong.

She spent lunchtime all alone,
All knotted up inside,
And after she got home
She fell across her bed and cried.

"I hate that school," she told her mom,
"I won't go back again!
How can I face another day
Without a single friend."

Her mother said,
"I love you, Jennifer,
No matter what you do,
And here's a little secret
I've come to learn is true.
If you try hard, you'll find happiness
In anything you do—
Or else you'll find it nowhere,
It's completely up to you."

Jennifer went back to school,
But it wasn't very nice,
For good things don't come easily
And patience is the price.

But soon she made some friends,
And as sunshine follows rain
Her life became so happy
She forgot about the pain.

She lived till she was ninety-six,
And on the day she died,
She called her great-great-grand kids
To sit down at her side.
She said,
"I love you, all my children,
No matter what you do,
So here's a little secret
I have come to learn is true.
If you try hard, you'll find happiness
In anything you do—
In the blossom-days of summer
Or when summertime is through,
In a velvet swing,
Or a wedding ring,
Or a worn-out leather shoe,
Or else you'll find it nowhere,
It's completely up to you."

The Life Song

You may think it'll never happen,
But it won't be long . . . you'll see.
Crystal age will come to you
As it has come to me.
For time is the voice that calls the leaf
To loosen from the tree
And float away on autumn air
In quiet reverie.
So greet the sun each morning
With spirit strong and free.
Meet the dawn as each day is born . . .
And become what you will be.